# YENTL THE YESHIVA BOY

ISAAC BASHEVIS SINGER

# yentl the yeshiva

# boy

Woodcuts by ANTONIO FRASCONI

FARRAR, STRAUS AND GIROUX · NEW YORK

Translated from the Yiddish
by Marion Magid and Elizabeth Pollet

Text copyright © 1962 by Isaac Bashevis Singer
Woodcuts copyright © 1983 by Antonio Frasconi
All rights reserved
Library of Congress catalog card number: 83-11620
Published simultaneously in Canada by Collins Publishers, Toronto
Printed in the United States of America
First edition, 1983

FTER HER
father's death, Yentl had no reason to remain in Yanev. She
was all alone in the house. To be sure, lodgers were willing
to move in and pay rent; and the marriage brokers flocked
to her door with offers from Lublin, Tomashev, Zamosc.
But Yentl didn't want to get married. Inside her, a voice
repeated over and over: "No!" What becomes of a girl
when the wedding's over? Right away she starts bearing
and rearing. And her mother-in-law lords it over her. Yentl
knew she wasn't cut out for a woman's life. She couldn't
sew, she couldn't knit. She let the food burn and the milk
boil over; her Sabbath pudding never turned out right, and
her hallah dough didn't rise. Yentl much preferred men's
activities to women's. Her father, Reb Todros, may he rest

in peace, during many bedridden years had studied Torah with his daughter as if she were a son. He told Yentl to lock the doors and drape the windows, then together they pored over the Pentateuch, the Mishnah, the Gemara, and the Commentaries.

She had proved so apt a pupil that her father used to say: "Yentl—you have the soul of a man."

"So why was I born a woman?"

"Even Heaven makes mistakes."

There was no doubt about it, Yentl was unlike any of the girls in Yanev—tall, thin, bony, with small breasts and narrow hips. On Sabbath afternoons, when her father slept, she would dress up in his trousers, his fringed garment, his silk coat, his skullcap, his velvet hat, and study her reflection in the mirror. She looked like a dark, handsome young man. There was even a slight down on her upper lip. Only her thick braids showed her womanhood—and if it came to that, hair could always be shorn. Yentl conceived a plan, and day and night she could think of nothing else. No, she had not been created for the noodle board and the pudding dish, for chattering with silly women and pushing for a place at the butcher's block. Her father had told her so many tales of yeshivas, rabbis, men of letters! Her head was full of Talmudic disputations, questions and answers, learned phrases. Secretly, she had even smoked her father's long pipe.

Yentl told the dealers she wanted to sell the house and go to live in Kalish with an aunt. The neighborhood women tried to talk her out of it, and the marriage brokers said she was crazy, that she was more likely to make a good match right here in Yanev. But Yentl was obstinate. She

was in such a rush that she sold the house to the first bid-
der, and let the furniture go for a song. All she realized
from her inheritance was one hundred and forty rubles.
Then, late one night in the month of Av, while Yanev slept,
Yentl cut off her braids, arranged sidelocks at her temples,
and dressed herself in her father's clothes. Packing underclothes, phylacteries, and a few books into a straw suitcase,
she started off on foot for Lublin.

On the main road, Yentl got a ride in a carriage that took
her as far as Zamosc. From there, she again set out on foot.
She stopped at an inn along the way, and gave her name
there as Anshel, after an uncle who had died. The inn was
crowded with young men journeying to study with famous
rabbis. An argument was in progress over the merits of
various yeshivas, some praising those of Lithuania, others
claiming that study was more intensive in Poland and the
board better. It was the first time Yentl had ever found herself alone in the company of young men. How different
their talk was from the jabbering of women, she thought,
but she was too shy to join in. One young man discussed a
prospective match and the size of the dowry, while another, parodying the manner of a Purim rabbi, declaimed a
passage from the Torah, adding all sorts of lewd interpre-
tations. After a while, the company proceeded to contests
of strength. One pried open another's fist; a second tried
to bend a companion's arm. One student, dining on bread
and tea, had no spoon and stirred his cup with his penknife.

Presently, one of the group came over to Yentl and poked
her in the shoulder. "Why so quiet? Don't you have a
tongue?"

"I have nothing to say."

"What's your name?"

"Anshel."

"You *are* bashful. A violet by the wayside."

And the young man tweaked Yentl's nose. She would have given him a smack in return, but her arm refused to budge. She turned white. Another student, slightly older than the rest, tall and pale, with burning eyes and a black beard, came to her rescue.

"Hey, you, why are you picking on him?"

"If you don't like it, you don't have to look."

"Want me to pull your sidelocks off?"

The bearded young man beckoned to Yentl, then asked where she came from and where she was going. Yentl told him she was looking for a yeshiva, but wanted a quiet one.

The young man pulled at his beard. "Then come with me to Bechev."

He explained that he was returning to Bechev for his fourth year. The yeshiva there was small, with only thirty students, and the people in the town provided board for them all. The food was plentiful and the housewives darned the students' socks and took care of their laundry. The Bechev rabbi, who headed the yeshiva, was a genius. He could pose ten questions and answer all ten with one proof. Most of the students eventually found wives in the town.

"Why did you leave in the middle of the term?" Yentl asked.

"My mother died. Now I'm on my way back."

"What's your name?"

"Avigdor."

"How is it you're not married?"

The young man scratched his beard. "It's a long story."

"Tell me."

Avigdor covered his eyes and thought a moment. "Are you coming to Bechev?"

"Yes."

"Then you'll find out soon enough anyway. I was engaged to the only daughter of Alter Vishkower, the richest man in town. Even the wedding date was set, when suddenly they sent back the engagement contract."

"What happened?"

"I don't know. Gossips, I guess, were busy spreading tales. I had the right to ask for half the dowry, but it was against my nature. Now they're trying to talk me into another match, but the girl doesn't appeal to me."

"In Bechev, yeshiva boys look at women?"

"At Alter's house, where I ate once a week, Hadass, his daughter, always brought in the food . . ."

"Is she good-looking?"

"She's blond."

"Brunettes can be good-looking too."

"No."

Yentl gazed at Avigdor. He was lean and bony, with sunken cheeks. He had curly sidelocks so black they appeared blue, and his eyebrows met across the bridge of his nose. He looked at her sharply with the regretful shyness of one who has just divulged a secret. His lapel was rent, according to the custom for mourners, and the lining of his gaberdine showed through. He drummed restlessly on the table and hummed a tune. Behind the high furrowed brow, his thoughts seemed to race.

Suddenly he spoke: "Well, what of it. I'll become a recluse, that's all."

It was strange, but as soon as Yentl—or Anshel—arrived in Bechev, she was allotted one day's board a week at the house of that same rich man, Alter Vishkower, whose daughter had broken off her betrothal to Avigdor.

The students at the yeshiva studied in pairs, and Avigdor chose Anshel for a partner. He helped her with the lessons. He was also an expert swimmer and offered to teach Anshel the breast stroke and how to tread water, but she always found excuses for not going down to the river. Avigdor

suggested that they share lodgings, but Anshel found a place to sleep at the house of an elderly widow who was half blind. Tuesdays, Anshel ate at Alter Vishkower's and Hadass waited on her. Avigdor always asked many questions: "How does Hadass look? Is she sad? Is she gay? Are they trying to marry her off? Does she ever mention my name?" Anshel reported that Hadass upset dishes on the tablecloth, forgot to bring the salt, and dipped her fingers into the plate of grits while carrying it. She ordered the servant girl around, was forever engrossed in storybooks, and changed her hairdo every week. Moreover, she must consider herself a beauty, for she was always in front of the mirror, but, in fact, she was not that good-looking.

"Two years after she's married," said Anshel, "she'll be an old bag."

"So she doesn't appeal to you?"

"Not particularly."

"Yet if she wanted you, you wouldn't turn her down."

"I can do without her."

"Don't you have evil impulses?"

The two friends, sharing a lectern in a corner of the study house, spent more time talking than learning. Occasionally Avigdor smoked, and Anshel, taking the cigarette from his lips, would have a puff. Avigdor liked baked flatcakes made with buckwheat, so Anshel stopped at the bakery every morning to buy one, and wouldn't let him pay his share. Often Anshel did things that greatly surprised Avigdor. If a button came off Avigdor's coat, for example, Anshel would arrive at the yeshiva the next day with needle and thread and sew it back on. Anshel bought Avigdor all kinds of presents: a silk handkerchief, a pair of socks, a muffler.

Avigdor grew more and more attached to this boy, five years younger than himself, whose beard hadn't even begun to sprout.

Once Avigdor said to Anshel: "I want you to marry Hadass."

"What good would that do *you*?"

"Better you than a total stranger."

"You'd become my enemy."

"Never."

Avigdor liked to go for walks through the town and Anshel frequently joined him. Engrossed in conversation, they would go off to the water mill, or to the pine forest, or to the crossroads where the Christian shrine stood. Sometimes they stretched out on the grass.

"Why can't a woman be like a man?" Avigdor asked once, looking up at the sky.

"How do you mean?"

"Why couldn't Hadass be just like you?"

"How like me?"

"Oh—a good fellow."

Anshel grew playful. She plucked a flower and tore off the petals one by one. She picked up a chestnut and threw it at Avigdor. Avigdor watched a ladybug crawl across the palm of his hand.

After a while he spoke up: "They're trying to marry me off."

Anshel sat up instantly. "To whom?"

"To Feitl's daughter, Peshe."

"The widow?"

"That's the one."

"Why should you marry a widow?"

"No one else will have me."

"That's not true. Someone will turn up for you."

"Never."

Anshel told Avigdor such a match was bad. Peshe was neither good-looking nor clever, only a cow with a pair of eyes. Besides, she was bad luck, for her husband died in the first year of their marriage. Such women were husband-killers. But Avigdor did not answer. He lit a cigarette, took a deep puff, and blew out smoke rings. His face had turned green.

"I need a woman. I can't sleep at night."

Anshel was startled. "Why can't you wait until the right one comes along?"

"Hadass was my destined one."

And Avigdor's eyes grew moist. Abruptly he got to his feet. "Enough lying around. Let's go."

After that, everything happened quickly. One day Avigdor was confiding his problem to Anshel, two days later he became engaged to Peshe, and brought honey cake and brandy to the yeshiva. An early wedding date was set. When the bride-to-be is a widow, there's no need to wait for a trousseau. Everything is ready. The groom, moreover, was an orphan and no one's advice had to be asked. The yeshiva students drank the brandy and offered their congratulations.

Anshel also took a sip, but promptly choked on it. "Oy, it burns!"

"You're not much of a man," Avigdor teased.

After the celebration, Avigdor and Anshel sat down with a volume of the Gemara, but they made little progress, and their conversation was equally slow. Avigdor rocked back and forth, pulled at his beard, muttered under his breath.

"I'm lost," he said abruptly.

"If you don't like her, why are you getting married?"

"I'd marry a she-goat."

The following day Avigdor did not appear at the study house. Feitl the leather dealer belonged to the Hasidim and he wanted his prospective son-in-law to continue his studies at the Hasidic prayer house. The yeshiva students said privately that though there was no denying the widow was short and round as a barrel, her mother the daughter of a dairyman, her father half an ignoramus, still the whole family was filthy with money. Feitl was part owner of a tannery; Peshe had invested her dowry in a shop that sold herring, tar, pots, and pans, and was always crowded with peasants. Father and daughter were outfitting Avigdor and had placed orders for a fur coat, a cloth coat, a silk kapote, and two pairs of boots. In addition, he had received many gifts immediately, things that had belonged to Peshe's first husband: the Vilna edition of the Talmud, a gold watch, a Hanukkah candelabrum, a spice box. Anshel sat alone at the lectern.

On Tuesday, when Anshel arrived for dinner at Alter Vishkower's house, Hadass remarked: "What do you say about your partner—back in clover, isn't he?"

"What did you expect—that no one else would want him?"

Hadass reddened. "It wasn't my fault. My father was against it."

"Why?"

"Because they found out a brother of his had hanged himself."

Anshel looked at her as she stood there—tall, blond, with a long neck, hollow cheeks, and blue eyes, wearing a cotton dress and a calico apron. Her hair, fixed in two braids, was flung back over her shoulders. A pity I'm not a man, Anshel thought.

"Do you regret it now?" Anshel asked.

"Oh, yes!"

Hadass fled from the room. The rest of the food, meat dumplings and tea, was brought in by the servant girl. Not until Anshel had finished eating and was washing her hands for the final blessings did Hadass reappear.

She came up to the table and said in a smothered voice: "Swear to me you won't tell him anything. Why should he know what goes on in my heart!"

Then she fled once more, nearly falling over the threshold.

Т he head of the yeshiva asked Anshel to choose another study partner, but weeks went by and still
Anshel studied alone. There was no one in the yeshiva who could take Avigdor's place. All the others were
small, in body and in spirit. They talked nonsense, bragged
about trifles, grinned oafishly, behaved like shnorrers.
Without Avigdor, the study house seemed empty. At
night, Anshel lay on her bench at the widow's, unable to
sleep. Stripped of gaberdine and trousers, she was once
more Yentl, a girl of marriageable age, in love with a young
man who was betrothed to another. Perhaps I should have
told him the truth, Anshel thought. But it was too late for
that. Anshel could not go back to being a girl, could never

again do without books and a study house. She lay there thinking outlandish thoughts that brought her close to madness. She fell asleep, then awoke with a start. In her dream she had been at the same time a man and a woman, wearing both a woman's bodice and a man's fringed garment. Yentl's period was late and she was suddenly afraid . . . who knew? In *Medrash Talpioth* she had read of a woman who had conceived merely through desiring a man. Only now did Yentl grasp the meaning of the Torah's prohibition against wearing the clothes of the other sex. By doing so, one deceived not only others but also oneself. Even the soul was perplexed, finding itself incarnate in a strange body.

At night, Anshel lay awake; by day, she could scarcely keep her eyes open. At the houses where she had her meals, the women complained that the youth left everything on his plate. The rabbi noticed that Anshel no longer paid attention to the lectures but stared out the window, lost in private thoughts. When Tuesday came, Anshel appeared at the Vishkower house for dinner. Hadass set a bowl of soup before her and waited, but Anshel was so disturbed she did not even say thank you. She reached for a spoon but let it fall.

Hadass ventured a comment: "I hear Avigdor has deserted you."

Anshel awoke from her trance. "What do you mean?"

"He's no longer your partner."

"He's left the yeshiva."

"Do you see him at all?"

"He seems to be hiding."

"Are you at least going to the wedding?"

For a moment Anshel was silent, as though missing the

meaning of the words. Then she spoke: "He's a big fool."

"Why do you say that?"

"You're beautiful, and the other one looks like a monkey."

Hadass blushed to the roots of her hair. "It's all my father's fault."

"Don't worry. You'll find someone who's worthy of you."

"There's no one I want."

"But everyone wants you . . ."

There was a long silence. Hadass's eyes grew larger, filling with the sadness of one who knows there is no consolation.

"Your soup is getting cold."

"I, too, want you."

Anshel was astonished at what she had said.

Hadass stared at her over her shoulder. "What are you saying!"

"It's the truth."

"Someone might be listening."

"I'm not afraid."

"Eat the soup. I'll bring the meat dumplings in a moment."

Hadass turned to go, her high heels clattering. Anshel began hunting for beans in the soup, fished one up, then let it fall. Her appetite was gone; her throat had closed up. She knew very well she was getting entangled in evil, but some force kept urging her on. Hadass reappeared, carrying a platter with two meat dumplings on it.

"Why aren't you eating?"

"I'm thinking about you."

"What are you thinking?"

"I want to marry you."

Hadass made a face as though she had swallowed something. "On such matters, you must speak to my father."

"I know."

"The custom is to send a matchmaker."

She ran from the room, letting the door slam behind her. Laughing inwardly, Anshel thought: With girls I can play as I please! She sprinkled salt on the soup, and then pepper. She sat there, light-headed. What have I done? I must be going mad. There's no other explanation . . . She forced herself to eat, but could taste nothing. Only then did Anshel remember that it was Avigdor who had wanted her to marry Hadass. From her confusion, a plan emerged: she would exact vengeance for Avigdor, and at the same time, through Hadass, draw him closer to herself. Hadass was a virgin: what did she know about men? A girl like that could be deceived for a long time. To be sure, Anshel too was a virgin, but she knew a lot about such matters from the Gemara and from hearing men talk. Anshel was seized by both fear and glee, as a person is who is planning to deceive the whole community. She remembered the saying: "The public are fools." She stood up and said aloud: "Now I'll really start something."

That night Anshel didn't sleep a wink. Every few minutes she got up for a drink of water. Her throat was parched, her forehead burned. Her brain worked away feverishly of its own volition. A quarrel seemed to be going on inside her. Her stomach throbbed and her knees ached. It was as if she had sealed a pact with Satan, the Evil One who plays tricks on human beings, who sets stumbling blocks and traps in their paths. By the time Anshel fell asleep, it was morning. She awoke more exhausted than before. But she could not go on sleeping on the bench at the widow's. With an effort she rose and, taking the bag that held her phylacteries, set out for the study house. On the way, whom should she meet but Hadass's father. Anshel bade him a respectful good morning and received a friendly greeting in return.

Reb Alter stroked his beard and engaged her in conversation. "My daughter Hadass must be serving you leftovers. You look starved."

"Your daughter is a fine girl, and very generous."

"So why are you so pale?"

Anshel was silent for a minute. "Reb Alter, there's something I must say to you."

"Well, go ahead, say it."

"Reb Alter, your daughter pleases me."

Alter Vishkower came to a halt. "Oh, does she? I thought yeshiva students didn't talk about such things." His eyes were full of laughter.

"But it's the truth."

"One doesn't discuss these matters with the young man himself."

"But I'm an orphan."

"Well . . . in that case, the custom is to send a marriage broker."

"Yes . . ."

"What do you see in her?"

"She's beautiful . . . fine . . . intelligent . . ."

"Well, well, well . . . Come along, tell me something about your family."

Alter Vishkower put his arm around Anshel and in this fashion the two continued walking until they reached the courtyard of the synagogue.

Once you say "A," you must say "B." Thoughts lead to words, words lead to deeds. Reb Alter Vishkower gave his consent to the match. Hadass's mother, Freyda Leah, held back for a while. She said she wanted no more Bechev yeshiva students for her daughter and would rather have someone from Lublin or Zamosc; but Hadass gave warning that if she was shamed publicly once more (the way she had been with Avigdor) she would throw herself into the well. As often happens with such ill-advised matches, everyone was strongly in favor of it—the rabbi, the relatives. Hadass's girl friends. For some time the girls of Bechev had been eyeing Anshel longingly, watching from their windows when the youth passed by on the street. Anshel kept his boots well polished and did not drop his eyes in the presence of women. Stopping in at Beila the baker's to buy a *pletzl*, he joked with them in such a worldly fashion that they marveled. The women agreed there was something special about Anshel: his sidelocks curled like nobody else's and he tied his neck scarf differently; his eyes, smiling yet distant, seemed always fixed on some faraway point. And the fact that Avigdor had become betrothed to Feitl's daughter Peshe, forsaking Anshel, had endeared him all the more to the people of the town. Alter Vishkower had a provisional contract drawn up for the betrothal, promising Anshel a bigger dowry, more presents, and an even longer period of maintenance than he had promised Avigdor. The girls of Bechev threw their arms around Hadass and congratulated her. Hadass immediately began crocheting a sack for Anshel's phylacteries, a hallah cloth, a matzoh bag. When Avigdor heard the news of Anshel's betrothal, he came to the study house to offer his congratulations. The past few weeks had aged him. His beard was disheveled, his eyes were red.

He said to Anshel: "I knew it would happen this way. Right from the beginning. As soon as I met you at the inn."

"But it was you who suggested it."

"I know that."

"Why did you desert me? You went away without even saying goodbye."

"I wanted to burn my bridges behind me."

Avigdor asked Anshel to go for a walk. Though it was already past Succoth, the day was bright with sunshine. Avigdor, friendlier than ever, opened his heart to Anshel.

Yes, it was true, a brother of his had succumbed to melancholy and hanged himself. Now he too felt himself near the edge of the abyss. Peshe had a lot of money and her father was a rich man, yet he couldn't sleep nights. He didn't want to be a storekeeper. He couldn't forget Hadass. She appeared in his dreams. Sabbath night, when her name occurred in the Havdala prayer, he turned dizzy. Still, it was good that Anshel and no one else was to marry her . . . At least she would fall into decent hands. Avigdor stooped and tore aimlessly at the shriveled grass. His speech was incoherent, like that of a man possessed.

Suddenly he said: "I have thought of doing what my brother did."

"Do you love her *that* much?"

"She's engraved in my heart."

The two pledged their friendship and promised never again to part. Anshel proposed that, after they were both married, they should live next door or even share the same house. They would study together every day, perhaps even become partners in a shop.

"Do you want to know the truth?" asked Avigdor. "It's like the story of Jacob and Benjamin: my life is bound up in your life."

"Then why did you leave me?"

"Perhaps for that very reason."

Though the day had turned cold and windy, they continued to walk until they reached the pine forest, not turning back until dusk, when it was time for the evening prayer. The girls of Bechev, from their posts at the windows, watched them going by with their arms around each other's shoulders and so engrossed in conversation that they walked through puddles and piles of trash without noticing. Avigdor looked pale, disheveled, and the wind whipped one sidelock about; Anshel chewed his fingernails. Hadass, too, ran to the window, took one look, and her eyes filled with tears.

Events followed quickly. Avigdor was the first to marry. Because the bride was a widow, the wedding was a quiet one, with no musicians, no wedding jester, no ceremonial veiling of the bride. One day Peshe stood beneath the marriage canopy, the next she was back at the shop, dispensing tar with greasy hands. Avigdor prayed at the Hasidic assembly house in his new prayer shawl. Afternoons, Anshel went to visit him and the two whispered and talked until evening. The date of Anshel's wedding to Hadass was set for the Sabbath in Hanukkah week, though the prospective father-in-law wanted it sooner. Hadass had already been betrothed once. Besides, the groom was an orphan. Why should he toss about on a makeshift bed at the widow's when he could have a wife and home of his own?

Many times each day, Anshel warned herself that what she was about to do was sinful, mad, an act of utter depravity. She was entangling both Hadass and herself in a chain of deception and committing so many transgressions that she would never be able to do penance. One lie followed another. Repeatedly, Anshel made up her mind to flee Bechev in time, to put an end to this weird comedy that was more the work of an imp than a human being. But she was in the grip of a power she could not resist. She grew more and more attached to Avigdor, and could not bring herself to destroy Hadass's illusory happiness. Now that he was married, Avigdor's desire to study was greater than ever, and the friends met twice each day: in the mornings they studied the Gemara and the Commentaries, in the afternoons the legal codes with their glosses. Alter Vishkower and Feitl the leather dealer were pleased and compared Avigdor and Anshel to David and Jonathan. With all the complications, Anshel went about as though drunk. The tailors took her measurements for a new wardrobe and she was forced into all kinds of subterfuge to keep them from discovering she was not a man. Though the imposture had lasted many weeks, Anshel still could not believe it: How was it possible? Fooling the community had become a game, but how long could it go on? And in what way would the truth come to the surface? Inside, Anshel laughed and wept. She had turned into a sprite brought into the world to mock people and trick them. I'm wicked, a transgressor, a Jeroboam ben Nabat, she told herself. Her only justification was that she had taken all these burdens upon herself because her soul thirsted to study Torah.

Avigdor soon began to complain that Peshe treated him badly. She called him an idler, a shlemiel, just another mouth to feed. She tried to tie him to the store, assigned him tasks for which he hadn't the slightest inclination, begrudged him pocket money. Instead of consoling Avigdor, Anshel goaded him on against Peshe. She called his wife an eyesore, a shrew, a miser, and said that Peshe had no doubt nagged her first husband to death and would Avigdor also. At the same time, Anshel enumerated Avigdor's virtues: his height and manliness, his wit, his erudition.

"If I were a woman and married to you," said Anshel, "I'd know how to appreciate you."

"Well, but you aren't . . ."

Avigdor sighed.

Meanwhile, Anshel's wedding date drew near.

On the Sabbath before Hanukkah, Anshel was called to the pulpit to read from the Torah. The women showered her with raisins and almonds. On the day of the wedding, Alter Vishkower gave a feast for the young men. Avigdor sat at Anshel's right hand. The bridegroom delivered a Talmudic discourse, and the rest of the company argued the points, while smoking cigarettes and drinking wine,

liqueurs, tea with lemon or raspberry jam. Then followed the ceremony of veiling the bride, after which the bridegroom was led to the wedding canopy that had been set up at the side of the synagogue. The night was frosty and clear, the sky full of stars. The musicians struck up a tune. Two rows of girls held lighted tapers and braided wax candles. After the wedding ceremony, the bride and groom broke their fast with golden chicken broth. Then the dancing began, and the announcement of the wedding gifts, all according to custom. The gifts were many and costly. The wedding jester depicted the joys and sorrows that were in store for the bride. Avigdor's wife, Peshe, was one of the guests, but though she was bedecked with jewels, she still looked ugly in a wig that sat low on her forehead, wearing an enormous fur cape, and with traces of tar on her hands that no amount of washing could ever remove. After the virtue dance, the bride and groom were led separately to the marriage chamber. The wedding attendants instructed the couple in the proper conduct and enjoined them to "be fruitful and multiply."

At daybreak, Anshel's mother-in-law and her band descended upon the marriage chamber and tore the bedsheets from beneath Hadass to make sure the marriage had been consummated. When traces of blood were discovered, the company grew merry and began kissing and congratulating the bride. Then, brandishing the sheet, they flocked outside and danced a kosher dance in the newly fallen snow. Anshel had found a way to deflower the bride. Hadass in her innocence was unaware that things weren't quite as they should have been. She was already deeply in love with Anshel. It is commanded that the bride and groom remain apart for seven days after the first intercourse. The next day Anshel and Avigdor took up the study of the Tractate on Menstruous Women. When the other men had departed and the two were left to themselves in the synagogue, Avigdor shyly questioned Anshel about his night with Hadass. Anshel gratified his curiosity and they whispered together until nightfall.

Anshel had fallen into good hands. Hadass was a devoted wife and her parents indulged their son-in-law's every wish and boasted of his accomplishments. To be sure, several months went by and Hadass was still not with child, but no one took it to heart. On the other hand, Avigdor's lot grew steadily worse. Peshe tormented him and finally would not give him enough to eat and even refused him a clean shirt. Since he was always penniless, Anshel again brought him a daily buckwheat cake. Because Peshe was too busy to cook and too stingy to hire a servant, Anshel asked Avigdor to dine at his house. Reb Alter Vishkower and his wife disapproved, arguing that it was wrong for the rejected suitor to visit the house of his former fiancée. The town had plenty to talk about. But Anshel cited precedents to show that it was not prohibited by the Law. Most of the townspeople sided with Avigdor and blamed Peshe for everything. Avigdor soon began pressing Peshe for a divorce, and because he did not want to have a child by such a fury, he acted like Onan, or, as the Gemara translates it, he threshed on the inside and cast his seed without. He confided in Anshel, told him how Peshe came to bed unwashed and snored like a buzz saw, how she was so occupied with the cash taken in at the store that she babbled about it even in her sleep.

"Oh, Anshel, how I envy you," he said.

"There's no reason for envying me."

"You have everything. I wish your good fortune were mine—with no loss to you, of course."

"Everyone has troubles of his own."

"What sort of troubles do *you* have? Don't tempt Providence."

How could Avigdor have guessed that Anshel could not sleep at night and thought constantly of running away? Lying with Hadass and deceiving her had become more and more painful. Hadass's love and tenderness shamed her. The devotion of her mother- and father-in-law and their hopes for a grandchild were a burden. On Friday afternoons, all the townspeople went to the baths, and every week Anshel had to find a new excuse. But this was beginning to

awake suspicions. There was talk that Anshel must have an unsightly birthmark, or a rupture, or perhaps was not properly circumcised. Judging by the youth's years, his beard should certainly have begun to sprout, yet his cheeks remained smooth. It was already Purim, and Passover was approaching. Soon it would be summer. Not far from Bechev, there was a river where all the yeshiva students and young men went swimming as soon as it was warm enough. The lie was swelling like an abscess and one of these days it must surely burst. Anshel knew she had to find a way to free herself.

It was customary for the young men boarding with their in-laws to travel to nearby cities during the half holidays in the middle of Passover week. They enjoyed the change, refreshed themselves, looked around for business opportunities, bought books or other things a young man might need. Bechev was not far from Lublin, and Anshel persuaded Avigdor to make the journey with her at her expense. Avigdor was delighted at the prospect of being rid for a few days of the shrew he had at home. The trip by carriage was a merry one. The fields were turning green; storks, back from the warm countries, swooped across the sky in great arcs. Streams rushed toward the valleys. The birds chirped. The windmills turned. Spring flowers were beginning to bloom in the fields. Here and there a cow was already grazing. The companions, chatting, ate the fruit and little cakes that Hadass had packed, told each other jokes, and exchanged confidences until they reached Lublin. There they went to an inn and took a room for two. During the journey, Anshel had promised to reveal an astonishing secret to Avigdor in Lublin. Avigdor had joked:

What sort of secret could it be? Had Anshel discovered a hidden treasure? Had he written an essay? By studying the Cabala, had he created a dove?

Now they entered the room, and while Anshel carefully locked the door, Avigdor said teasingly: "Well, let's hear your great secret."

"Prepare yourself for the most incredible thing that ever was."

"I'm prepared for anything."

"I'm not a man but a woman," said Anshel. "My name isn't Anshel, it's Yentl."

Avigdor burst out laughing. "I knew it was a hoax."

"But it's true."

"Even if I'm a fool, I won't swallow this."

"Do you want me to show you?"

"Yes."

"Then I'll get undressed."

Avigdor's eyes widened. It occurred to him that Anshel might want to practice pederasty. Anshel took off the gaberdine and the fringed garment, and threw off her underclothes. Avigdor took one look and turned first white, then fiery red. Anshel covered herself hastily.

"I've done this only so that you can testify at the courthouse. Otherwise, Hadass will have to stay a grass widow."

Avigdor had lost his tongue. He was seized by a fit of trembling. He wanted to speak, but his lips moved and nothing came out. He sat down quickly, for his legs would not support him.

Finally he murmured: "How is it possible? I don't believe it!"

"Should I get undressed again?"

"No!"

Yentl proceeded to tell the whole story: how her father, bedridden, had studied Torah with her; how she had never had the patience for women and their silly chatter; how she had sold the house and all the furnishings, left the town, made her way disguised as a man to Lublin, and on the road met Avigdor. Avigdor sat speechless, gazing at the storyteller. Yentl was by now wearing men's clothes once more.

Avigdor spoke: "It must be a dream." He pinched himself on the cheek.

"It isn't a dream."

"That such a thing should happen to me!"

"It's all true."

"Why did you do it? *Nu*, I'd better keep still."

"I didn't want to waste my life on a baking shovel and a kneading trough."

"And what about Hadass—why did you do that?"

"I did it for your sake. I knew that Peshe would torment you and at our house you would have some peace."

Avigdor was silent for a long time. He bowed his head, pressed his hands to his temples, shook his head. "What will you do now?"

"I'll go away to a different yeshiva."

"What? If you had only told me earlier, we could have . . ." Avigdor broke off in the middle.

"No—it wouldn't have been good."

"Why not?"

"I'm neither one nor the other."

"What a dilemma I'm in!"

"Get a divorce from that horror. Marry Hadass."

"She'll never divorce me and Hadass won't have me."

"Hadass loves you. She won't listen to her father again."

Avigdor stood up suddenly but then sat down. "I won't be able to forget you. Ever . . ."

Acording to the Law, Avigdor was now forbidden to spend another moment alone with Yentl; yet, dressed in the gaberdine and trousers, she was again the familiar Anshel.

They resumed their conversation on the old footing: "How could you bring yourself to violate the commandment every day: 'A woman shall not wear that which pertaineth to a man'?"

"I wasn't created for plucking feathers and chattering with females."

"Would you rather lose your share in the world to come?"

"Perhaps . . ."

Avigdor raised his eyes. Only now did he realize that Anshel's cheeks were too smooth for a man's, the hair too abundant, the hands too small. Even so, he could not believe that such a thing could have happened. At any moment he expected to wake up. He bit his lips, pinched his thigh. He was seized by shyness and could not speak without stammering. His friendship with Anshel, their intimate talk, their confidences, had been turned into a sham and a delusion. The thought even occurred to him that Anshel might be a demon. He shook himself as if to cast off a nightmare; yet that power which knows the difference between dream and reality told him it was all true. He summoned up his courage. He and Anshel could never be strangers to one another, even though Anshel was in fact Yentl . . .

He ventured a comment: "It seems to me that the witness who testifies for a deserted woman may not marry her, for the Law calls him 'a party to the affair.' "

"What? That didn't occur to me!"

"We must look it up in Eben Ezer."

"I'm not even sure that the rules pertaining to a deserted woman apply in this case," said Anshel in the manner of a scholar.

"If you don't want Hadass to be a grass widow, you must reveal the secret to her directly."

"That I can't do."

"In any event, you must get another witness."

Gradually, the two went back to their Talmudic conversation. It seemed strange at first to Avigdor to be disputing holy writ with a woman, yet before long the Torah had reunited them. Though their bodies were different, their souls were of one kind. Anshel spoke in a singsong, gesticulated with her thumb, clutched her sidelocks, plucked at her beardless chin, made all the customary gestures of a yeshiva student. In the heat of argument, she even seized Avigdor by the lapel and called him stupid. A great love for Anshel took hold of Avigdor, mixed with shame, remorse, anxiety. If I had only known this before, he said to himself. In his thoughts he likened Anshel (or Yentl) to Bruria, the wife of Reb Meir, and to Yalta, the wife of Reb Nachman. For the first time he saw clearly that this was what he had always wanted: a wife whose mind was not taken up with material things . . . His desire for Hadass was gone now, and he knew he would long for Yentl, but he dared not say so. He felt hot and knew that his face was burning. He could no longer meet Anshel's eyes. He began to enumerate Anshel's sins and saw that he too was implicated, for he had sat next to Yentl and had touched her during her unclean days. *Nu*, and what could be said about her marriage to Hadass? What a multitude of transgressions there! Willful deception, false vows, misrepresentation!–Heaven knows what else.

He asked suddenly: "Tell the truth, are you a heretic?"

"God forbid!"

"Then how could you bring yourself to do such a thing?"

The longer Anshel talked, the less Avigdor understood. All Anshel's explanations seemed to point to one thing: she had the soul of a man and the body of a woman. Anshel said she had married Hadass only in order to be near Avigdor.

"You could have married me," Avigdor said.

"I wanted to study the Gemara and Commentaries with you, not darn your socks!"

For a long time neither spoke. Then Avigdor broke the silence: "I'm afraid Hadass will get sick from all this, God forbid!"

"I'm afraid of that, too."

"What's going to happen now?"

Dusk fell and the two began to recite the evening prayer. In his confusion Avigdor mixed up the blessings, omitted some and repeated others. He glanced sideways at Anshel, who was rocking back and forth, beating her breast, bowing her head. He saw her, eyes closed, lift her face to

Heaven, as though beseeching: You, Father in Heaven, know the truth . . . When their prayers were finished, they sat down on opposite chairs, facing one another yet a good distance apart. The room filled with shadows. Reflections of the sunset, like purple embroidery, shook on the wall opposite the window. Avigdor again wanted to speak, but at first the words, trembling on the tip of his tongue, would not come.

Suddenly they burst forth: "Maybe it's still not too late? I can't go on living with that accursed woman . . . You . . ."

"No, Avigdor, it's impossible."

"Why?"

"I'll live out my time as I am . . ."

"I'll miss you. Terribly."

"And I'll miss you."

"What's the sense of all this?"

Anshel did not answer. Night fell and the light faded. In the darkness they seemed to be listening to each other's thoughts. The Law forbade Avigdor to stay in the room alone with Anshel, but he could not think of her just as a woman. What a strange power there is in clothing, he thought.

But he spoke of something else: "I would advise you simply to send Hadass a divorce."

"How can I do that?"

"Since the marriage sacraments weren't valid, what difference does it make?"

"I suppose you're right."

"There'll be time enough later for her to find out the truth."

The maidservant came in with a lamp, but as soon as she

had gone, Avigdor put it out. Their predicament and the words which they must speak to one another could not endure light. In the blackness, Anshel related all the particulars. She answered all Avigdor's questions. The clock struck two, and still they talked. Anshel told Avigdor that Hadass had never forgotten him. She talked of him frequently, worried about his health, was sorry–though not without a certain satisfaction–about the way things had turned out with Peshe.

"She'll be a good wife," said Anshel. "I don't even know how to bake a pudding."

"Nevertheless, if you're willing . . ."

"No, Avigdor. It wasn't destined to be . . ."

It was all a great riddle to the town: the messenger who arrived bringing Hadass the divorce papers; Avigdor's remaining in Lublin until after the holidays; his return to Bechev with slumping shoulders and lifeless eyes as if he had been ill. Hadass took to her bed and was visited by the doctor three times a day. Avigdor went into seclusion. If someone ran across him by chance and addressed him, he did not answer. Peshe complained to her parents that Avigdor paced back and forth, smoking all night long. When he finally collapsed from sheer fatigue, in his sleep he called out the name of an unknown female—Yentl. Peshe began talking of a divorce. The town thought Avigdor wouldn't grant her one or would demand money at the very least, but he agreed to everything.

In Bechev, the people were not used to having mysteries

stay mysteries for long. How can you keep secrets in a little town where everyone knows what's cooking in everyone else's pots? Yet, though there were plenty of persons who made a practice of looking through keyholes and laying an ear to shutters, what happened remained an enigma. Hadass lay in her bed and wept. Chanina the herb doctor reported that she was wasting away. Anshel had disappeared without a trace. Reb Alter Vishkower sent for Avigdor and he arrived, but those who stood straining beneath the window couldn't catch a word of what passed between them. Those individuals who habitually pry into other people's affairs came up with all sorts of theories, but not one of them was consistent.

One party came to the conclusion that Anshel had fallen into the hands of Catholic priests and had been converted. That might have made sense. But where could Anshel have found time for the priests, since he was always studying in the yeshiva? And, apart from that, since when does an apostate send his wife a divorce?

Another group whispered that Anshel had cast an eye on another woman. But who could it be? There were no love affairs conducted in Bechev. And none of the young women had recently left town—neither a Jewish woman nor a Gentile one.

Somebody else offered the suggestion that Anshel had been carried away by evil spirits, or was even one of them himself. As proof he cited the fact that Anshel had never come either to the bathhouse or to the river. It is well known that demons have the feet of geese. Well, but had Hadass never seen him barefoot? And who ever heard of a demon sending his wife a divorce? When a demon marries a daughter of mortals, he usually lets her remain a grass widow.

It occurred to someone else that Anshel had committed a major transgression and gone into exile in order to do penance. But what sort of transgression could it have been? And why had he not entrusted it to the rabbi? And why did Avigdor wander about like a ghost?

The hypothesis of Tevel the musician was closest to the truth. Tevel maintained that Avigdor had been unable to forget Hadass and that Anshel had divorced her so that his friend would be able to marry her. But was such friendship possible in this world? And in that case, why had Anshel divorced Hadass even before Avigdor divorced Peshe? Furthermore, such a thing can be accomplished only if the wife has been informed of the arrangement and is willing, yet all signs pointed to Hadass's great love for Anshel, and in fact she was ill from sorrow.

One thing was clear to all: Avigdor knew the truth. But it was impossible to get anything out of him. He remained in seclusion and kept silent with an obstinacy that was a re-proof to the whole town.

Close friends urged Peshe not to divorce Avigdor, though they had severed all relations and no longer lived as man and wife. He did not even, on Friday night, perform the kiddush blessing for her. He spent his nights either at the study house or at the widow's where Anshel had found lodgings. When Peshe spoke to him he didn't answer, but stood with bowed head. The tradeswoman Peshe had no patience for such goings-on. She needed a young man to help her out in the store, not a yeshiva student who had fallen into melancholy. Someone of that sort might even

take it into his head to depart and leave her deserted. Peshe agreed to a divorce.

In the meantime, Hadass had recovered, and Reb Alter Vishkower let it be known that a marriage contract was being drawn up. Hadass was to marry Avigdor. The town was agog. A marriage between a man and a woman who had once been engaged and their betrothal broken off was unheard of. The wedding was held on the first Sabbath after Tishe b'Av, and included all that is customary at the marriage of a virgin: the banquet for the poor, the canopy before the synagogue, the musicians, the wedding jester, the virtue dance. Only one thing was lacking: joy. The bridegroom stood beneath the marriage canopy, a figure of desolation. The bride had recovered from her sickness, but had remained pale and thin. Her tears fell into the golden chicken broth. From all eyes the same question looked out: Why had Anshel done it?

After Avigdor's marriage to Hadass, Peshe spread the rumor that Anshel had sold his wife to Avigdor for a price, and that the money had been supplied by Alter Vishkower. One young man pondered the riddle at great length until he finally arrived at the conclusion that Anshel had lost his beloved wife to Avigdor at cards, or even on a spin of the Hanukkah dreidl. It is a general rule that when the grain of truth cannot be found, men will swallow great helpings of falsehood. Truth itself is often concealed in such a way that the harder you look for it, the harder it is to find.

Not long after the wedding, Hadass became pregnant. The child was a boy, and those assembled at the circumcision could scarcely believe their ears when they heard the father name his son Anshel.

# Notes on the Woodcuts

*Pages 3 and 5* | Details from an ancient tile depicting the sacrifice of Isaac.

*Page 13* | A modern version of a traditional paper cut displayed in the window during Shavuot. It incorporates a menorah, the tree of life, birds, animals, and flowers.

*Page 21* | A modern tile, based on an old mosaic floor pattern, depicting a menorah, a shofar, and an ethrog.

*Page 27* | An eighteenth-century Torah curtain.

*Page 32* | A communal wedding ring, side view and front view.

*Page 35* | A sixteenth-century wall hanging appliquéd on an eighteenth-century Torah curtain.

*Page 38* | An eighteenth-century "Elijah cup," set at the Prophet Elijah's place at the Passover Seder.

*Page 51* | An eighteenth-century spice container, used in the havdalah ceremony.

*Page 54* | Torah pointers terminating in the shape of a human hand.

*Page 60* | A brass cup.

*Page 63* | A nineteenth-century spice container, used in the havdalah ceremony.

The text of this book was set in Emerson Monotype
by A. Colish, Inc. The book was designed by
Antonio Frasconi, printed by Rembrandt Press, Inc.,
and bound by A. Horowitz and Sons.